THREE LITTLE PIGS

A FAVORITE STORY IN RHYTHM AND RHYME

Retold by SUSAN SANDVIG WALKER

Illustrated by MAXIME LEBRUN

Music Arranged and Produced by DREW TEMPERANTE

CANTATA
LEARNING

WWW.CANTATALEARNING.COM

CANTATA LEARNING

Published by Cantata Learning
1710 Roe Crest Drive
North Mankato, MN 56003
www.cantatalearning.com

A note to educators and librarians from the publisher: Cantata Learning has provided the following data to assist in book processing and suggested use of Cantata Learning product.

Publisher's Cataloging-in-Publication Data
Prepared by Librarian Consultant: Ann-Marie Begnaud
Library of Congress Control Number: 2015958174
    Three Little Pigs : A Favorite Story in Rhythm and Rhyme
    Series: Fairy Tale Tunes
    Retold by Susan Sandvig Walker
    Illustrated by Maxime LeBrun
    Summary: The classic fairy tale of the Three Little Pigs comes to life with music and full-color illustrations.
    ISBN: 978-1-63290-553-6 (library binding/CD)
    ISBN: 978-1-63290-654-0 (paperback/CD)
Suggested Dewey and Subject Headings:
    Dewey: E 398.2
    LCSH Subject Headings: Animals – Folklore – Juvenile literature. | Pigs – Folklore – Juvenile literature. | Animals – Folklore – Songs and music – Texts. | Pigs – Folklore – Songs and music – Texts. | Animals – Folklore – Juvenile sound recordings. | Pigs – Folklore – Juvenile sound recordings.
    Sears Subject Headings: Animals – Folklore. | Pigs – Folklore. | School songbooks. | Children's songs. | Popular music.
    BISAC Subject Headings: JUVENILE FICTION / Fairy Tales & Folklore / Adaptations. | JUVENILE FICTION / Stories in Verse. | JUVENILE FICTION / Animals / Pigs.

Book design and art direction, Tim Palin Creative
Editorial direction, Flat Sole Studio
Music direction, Elizabeth Draper
Music arranged and produced by Drew Temperante

Printed in the United States of America in North Mankato, Minnesota.
072016   0335CGF16

ACCESS THE MUSIC!

SCAN CODE WITH MOBILE APP

CANTATALEARNING.COM

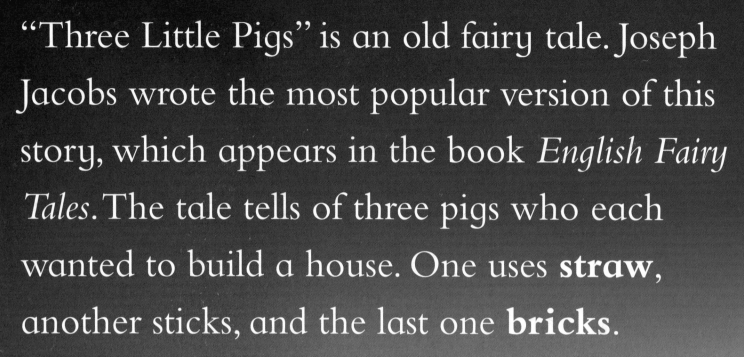

"Three Little Pigs" is an old fairy tale. Joseph Jacobs wrote the most popular version of this story, which appears in the book *English Fairy Tales*. The tale tells of three pigs who each wanted to build a house. One uses **straw**, another sticks, and the last one **bricks**.

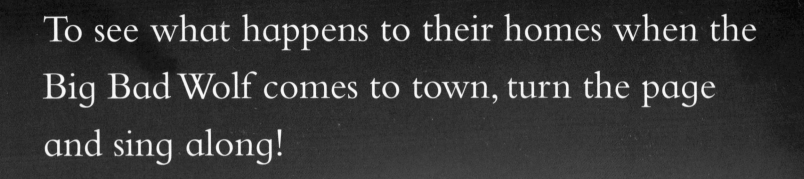

To see what happens to their homes when the Big Bad Wolf comes to town, turn the page and sing along!

Three little pigs, so nice and round,
built three homes on the edge of town.

Oh, they were Hippy, Hoppy, and Happy,
thinking they were safe and sound.

One house of straw, and one of sticks,
and one big house just made of bricks.

The pigs were Hippy, Hoppy, and Happy
until that wolf got in the mix.

The Big Bad Wolf would not listen, smiling with his **sneaky** grin.

The wolf knocked, and he knocked some more.
He **huffed** and puffed, blowing in the door.

The house of straw just fell to pieces,
and one little pig ran next door.

13

The Big Bad Wolf would not listen,
smiling with his sneaky grin.

The wolf knocked, and he knocked some more.
He huffed and puffed, blowing in the door.

The house of sticks crashed all around,
and two little pigs ran next door.

Again he huffed and puffed some more.
The wolf tried blowing down the door.

That brick house was strong and **sturdy**.
The pigs were laughing on the floor.

Those little pigs didn't let him in,
not by the hair of their chinny chin chins.

The big brick house was safe and sound,
and the pigs wouldn't be scared again.

SONG LYRICS
Three Little Pigs

Three little pigs, so nice and round,
built three homes on the edge of town.

Oh, they were Hippy, Hoppy, and Happy,
thinking they were safe and sound.

One house of straw, and one of sticks,
and one big house just made of bricks.

The pigs were Hippy, Hoppy, and Happy
until that wolf got in the mix.

"Oh, little pig, please let me in!"
"Not by the hair of my chinny chin chin!"

The Big Bad Wolf would not listen,
smiling with his sneaky grin.

The wolf knocked, and he knocked some more.
He huffed and puffed, blowing in the door.

The house of straw just fell to pieces,
and one little pig ran next door.

"Oh, little pig, please let me in!"
"Not by the hair of my chinny chin chin!"

The Big Bad Wolf would not listen,
smiling with his sneaky grin.

The wolf knocked, and he knocked some more.
He huffed and puffed, blowing in the door.

The house of sticks crashed all around,
and two little pigs ran next door.

Again he huffed and puffed some more.
The wolf tried blowing down the door.

That brick house was strong and sturdy.
The pigs were laughing on the floor.

Those little pigs didn't let him in,
not by the hair of their chinny chin chins.

The big brick house was safe and sound,
and the pigs wouldn't be scared again.

Three Little Pigs

Hip Hop
Drew Temperante

Verse

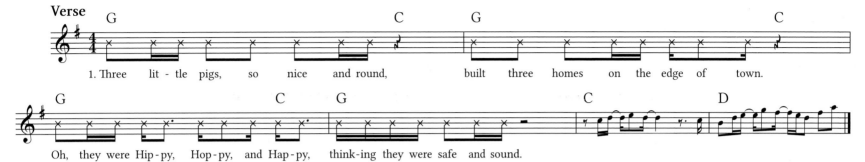

1. Three lit - tle pigs, so nice and round, built three homes on the edge of town.

Oh, they were Hip-py, Hop-py, and Hap-py, think-ing they were safe and sound.

Verse 2
One house of straw, and one of sticks,
and one big house just made of bricks.
The pigs were Hippy, Hoppy, and Happy
until that wolf got in the mix.

Verse 3
"Oh, little pig, please let me in!"
"Not by the hair of my chinny chin chin!"
The Big Bad Wolf would not listen,
smiling with his sneaky grin.

Chorus

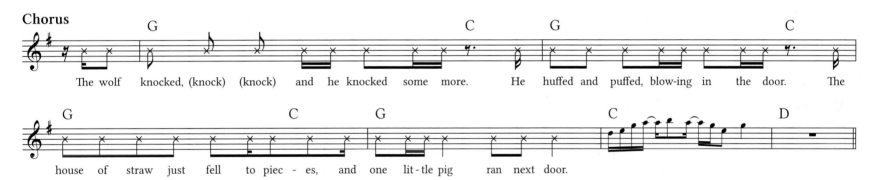

The wolf knocked, (knock) (knock) and he knocked some more. He huffed and puffed, blow-ing in the door. The

house of straw just fell to piec - es, and one lit - tle pig ran next door.

Verse 4
"Oh, little pig, please let me in!"
"Not by the hair of my chinny chin chin!"
The Big Bad Wolf would not listen,
smiling with his sneaky grin.

Verse 5
Again he huffed and puffed some more.
The wolf tried blowing down the door.
That brick house was strong and sturdy.
The pigs were laughing on the floor.

Chorus
The wolf knocked, and he knocked some more.
He huffed and puffed, blowing in the door.
The house of sticks crashed all around,
and two little pigs ran next door.

Verse 6
Those little pigs didn't let him in,
not by the hair of their chinny chin chins.
The big brick house was safe and sound,
and the pigs wouldn't be scared again.

ACCESS THE MUSIC!
SCAN CODE WITH MOBILE APP
CANTATALEARNING.COM

23

GLOSSARY

bricks—blocks of hard-baked clay used for building

huffed—to have breathed out puffs of air

sneaky—tricky or dishonest

straw—dried stems of wheat, barley, or oat plants

sturdy—strong and firm

GUIDED READING ACTIVITIES

1. The three pigs each chose a different material to build a house: straw, sticks, and bricks. Can you think of one good and one bad thing about each type of material?

2. If you could build your own house, what would it look like? Draw a picture of it.

3. Look at the picture of the pigs on page 20. How do you think they are feeling? Have you ever felt that way and why?

TO LEARN MORE

Jewitt, Kath. *The Three Little Pigs*. New York: Parragon, 2015.

Maccarone, Grace. *Three Little Pigs Count to 100*. Chicago: Albert Whitman, 2015.

Sommer, Carl. *Three Little Pigs*. Houston: Advance Publishing, 2014.

York, M. J. *Three Little Pigs*. Mankato, MN: Child's World, 2013.